Dear Parent:
Your child's love of reading starts here!

Every child learns to read in a different way and at his or her own speed. Some go back and forth between reading levels and read favorite books again and again. Others read through each level in order. You can help your young reader improve and become more confident by encouraging his or her own interests and abilities. From books your child reads with you to the first books he or she reads alone, there are I Can Read Books for every stage of reading:

SHARED READING
Basic language, word repetition, and whimsical illustrations, ideal for sharing with your emergent reader

BEGINNING READING
Short sentences, familiar words, and simple concepts for children eager to read on their own

READING WITH HELP
Engaging stories, longer sentences, and language play for developing readers

READING ALONE
Complex plots, challenging vocabulary, and high-interest topics for the independent reader

ADVANCED READING
Short paragraphs, chapters, and exciting themes for the perfect bridge to chapter books

I Can Read Books have introduced children to the joy of reading since 1957. Featuring award-winning authors and illustrators and a fabulous cast of beloved characters, I Can Read Books set the standard for beginning readers.

A lifetime of discovery begins with the magical words **"I Can Read!"**

Visit www.icanread.com for information
on enriching your child's reading experience.

I Can Read Book® is a trademark of HarperCollins Publishers.

Winter Wasteland
Copyright © 2015 DC Comics.
BATMAN and all related characters and elements are trademarks of and © DC Comics.
(s15)

HARP30665

Library of Congress catalog card number: 2014934803
ISBN 978-0-06-221004-3

Book design by Joe Merkel

15 16 17 18 19   SCP   10 9 8 7 6 5 4 3 2 1   ❖   First Edition

I Can Read!

READING 2 WITH HELP

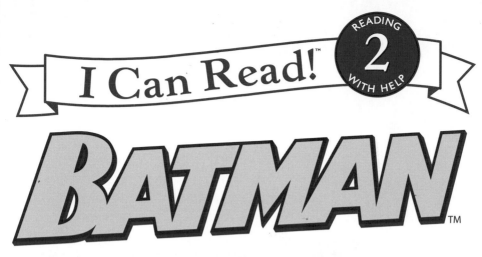

BATMAN™

Winter Wasteland

by Donald Lemke
pictures by Steven E. Gordon
colors by Eric A. Gordon

Batman created by Bob Kane

HARPER
An Imprint of HarperCollinsPublishers

BRUCE WAYNE

Bruce is a rich businessman. Orphaned as a child, he trained his body and mind to become Batman, the Dark Knight.

BATMAN

Batman is an expert martial artist, crime fighter, and inventor. He is known as the World's Greatest Detective.

ALFRED PENNYWORTH

Alfred is Bruce Wayne's loyal butler. He knows Bruce is secretly Batman and helps his crime-fighting efforts.

THE FLASH

The Flash is also known as Barry Allen. A research accident gave this professor the lightning-quick abilities of The Flash, the Fastest Man Alive.

WONDER WOMAN

Wonder Woman, also known as Princess Diana, was born on Paradise Island. She has incredible strength and flies an Invisible Jet.

THE ICE PACK

The Ice Pack is a group of frosty felons, which includes Captain Cold, Mr. Freeze, and Killer Frost. They each have subzero powers and weapons.

On a humid July day, Bruce Wayne
sat on a porch outside his mansion.
He took the final sip of iced tea
from his glass.

"Care for more?" asked his butler.

"Thank you, Alfred," Bruce replied.
Suddenly, a dime-sized snowflake
landed on Bruce's hand.
"How odd," said Alfred, puzzled.

Soon a thin layer of snow covered the lawn.

Bruce quickly headed to his top secret hideout, which contained the weapons, gadgets, and uniform of Bruce's secret identity, Batman.

On the Batcomputer,

a breaking news story

reported a midsummer blizzard.

"The Ice Pack," Batman grumbled,

knowing this chilly trio was back.

Batman sped through the snowy streets

inside the Batmobile.

When he arrived in Gotham City,

he spotted his coldest enemy,

Mr. Freeze.

The frozen felon fired icy blasts

at nearby buildings.

"Stop right there!" shouted Batman.

The villain turned and smiled.

"Don't you mean freeze?" he asked.

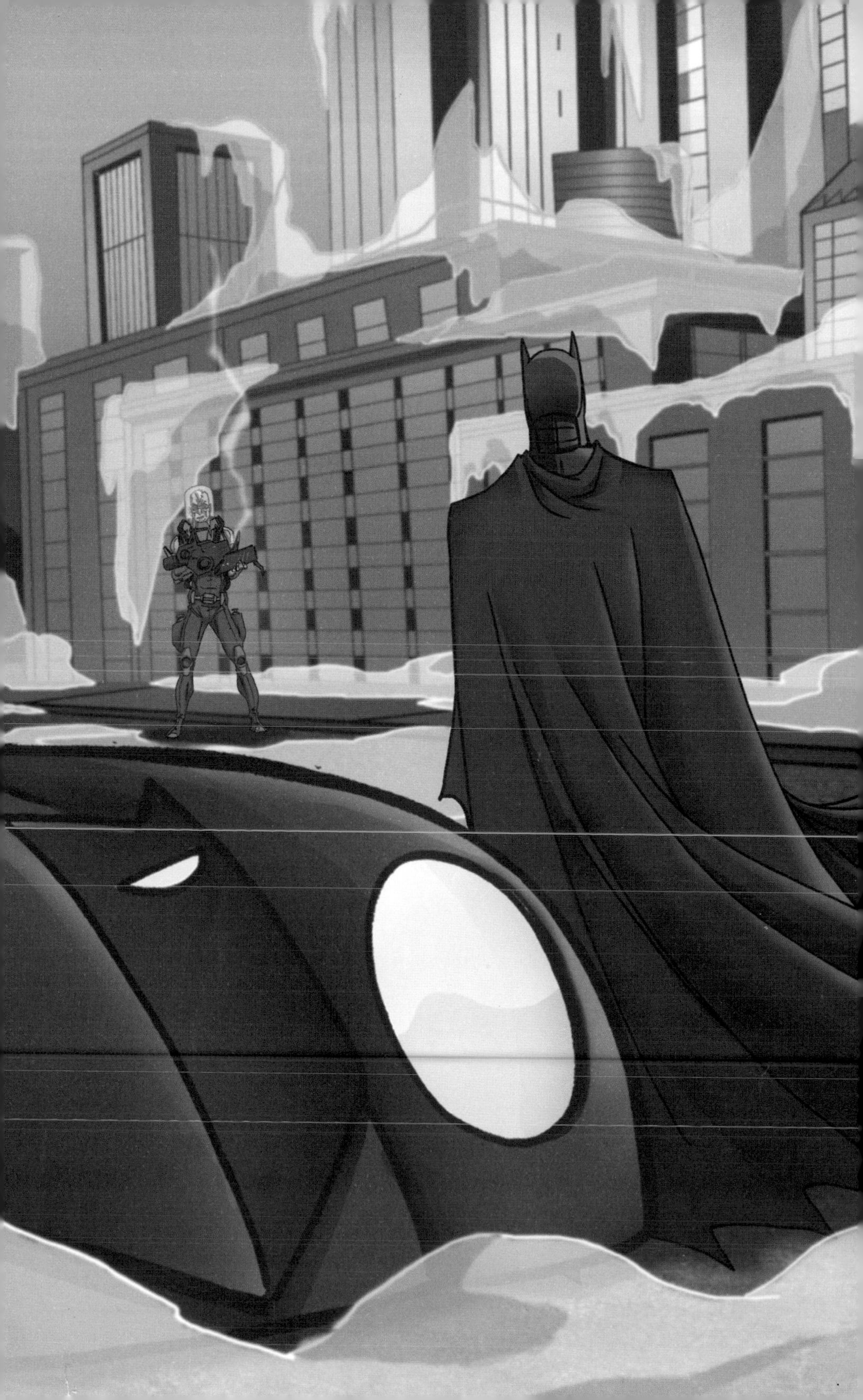

Mr. Freeze fired at Batman.
BZZZT!
Using his martial arts skills,
the hero flipped out of the way.
More blasts came from above,
exploding at Batman's feet.

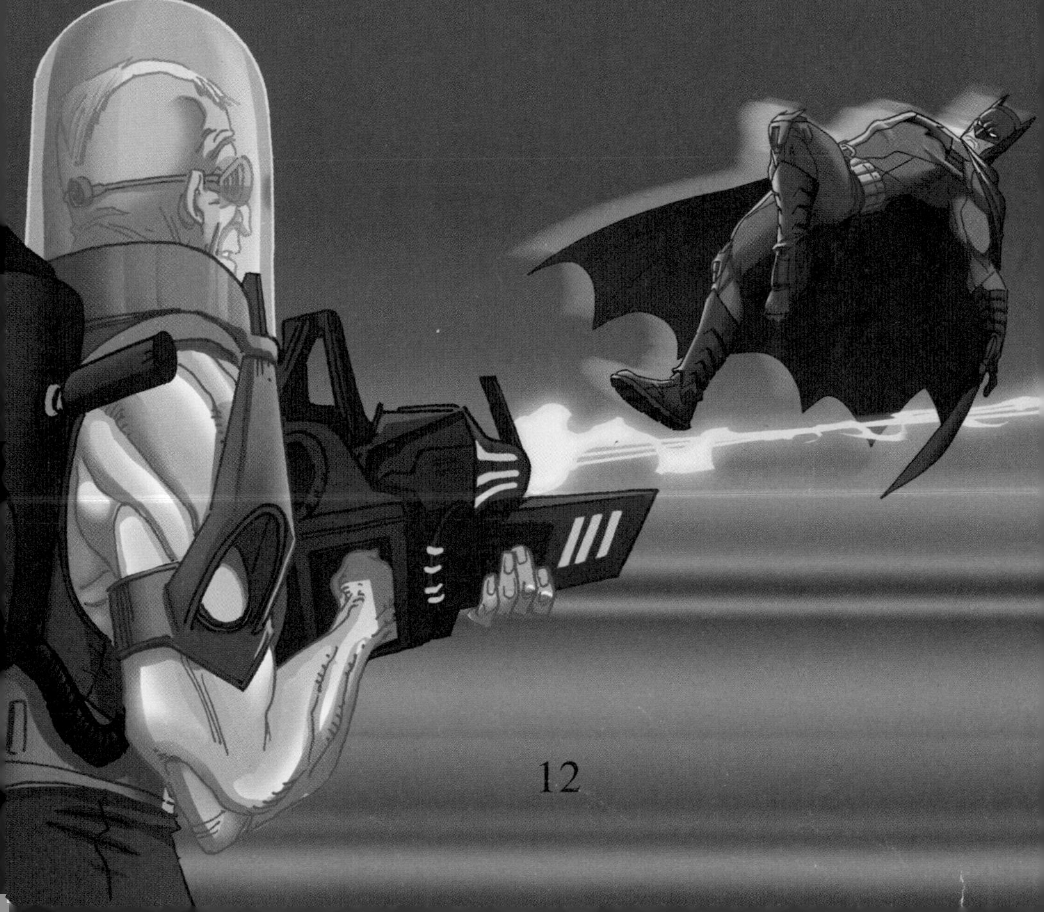

On a nearby rooftop stood
two other members of the Ice Pack,
Captain Cold and Killer Frost.
"We're sending Gotham back
to the Ice Age," said Captain Cold.

The villains shot their weapons.
The Dark Knight spun, jumped,
and flipped to avoid the attack.
Finally Batman dived for safety
inside the armored Batmobile.

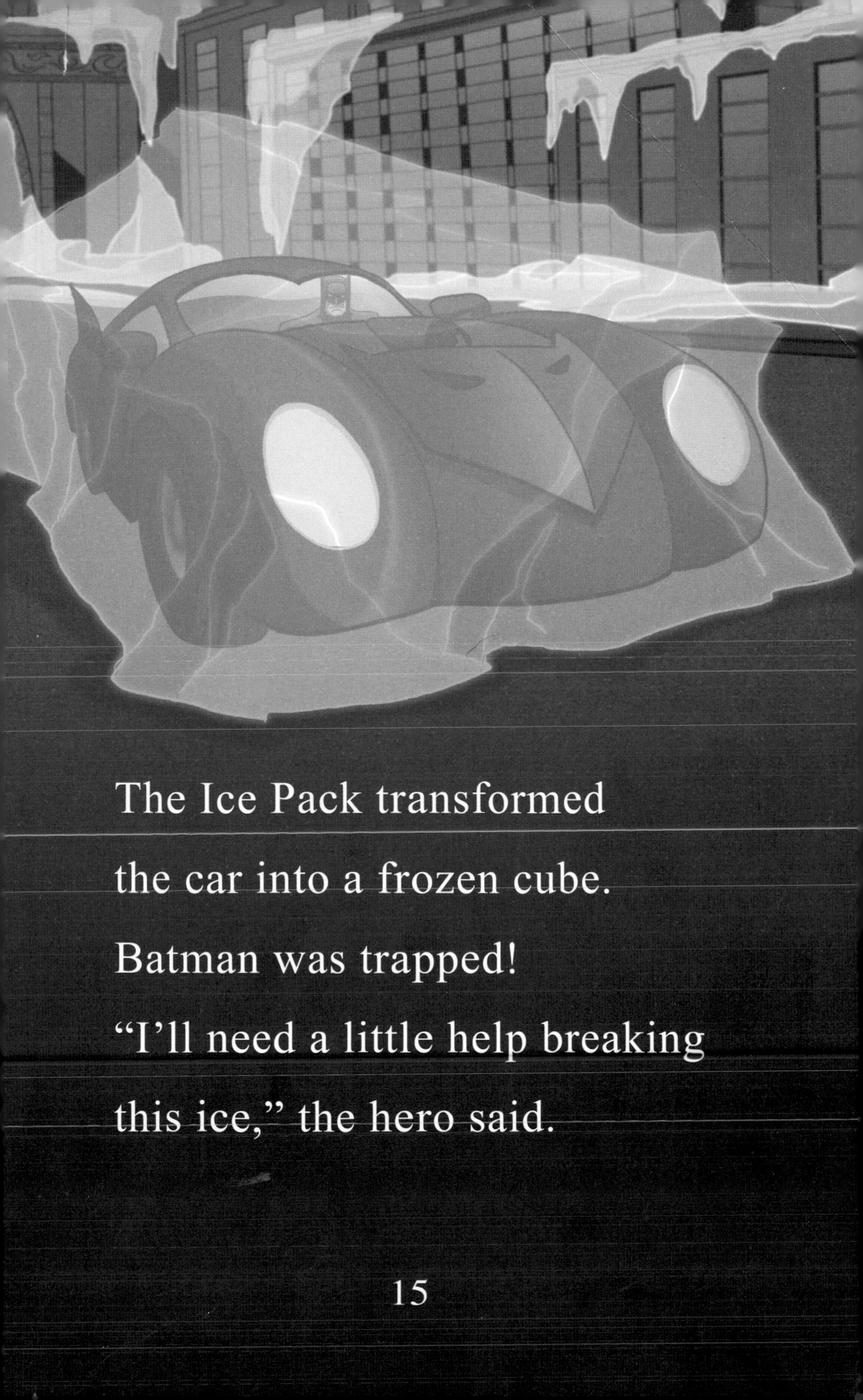

The Ice Pack transformed
the car into a frozen cube.
Batman was trapped!
"I'll need a little help breaking
this ice," the hero said.

Batman pressed a button
in the Batmobile.
A red-and-yellow blur
streaked toward him.
The Flash!

The Fastest Man Alive ran
circles around the Batmobile,
creating a swirling tornado of heat.
The ice covering the vehicle melted.
"What took so long?" Batman joked.

"We have company," said Batman, pointing at the chilly trio.

"Give up, Cold," The Flash said.

"This Ice Age is over."

"Not a snowball's chance," said the villain.

He fired cannonballs of snow.

The Flash twirled his arms

at top speed, creating a shield of heat.

The snowballs melted in midair!

Through the steam of melting snow,

Wonder Woman landed

on the streets of Gotham City.

Killer Frost greeted her

with a flurry of razor-sharp icicles.

Wonder Woman blocked

the ice with her silver bracelets.

"So much for a warm welcome,"

she said, joining her fellow heroes.

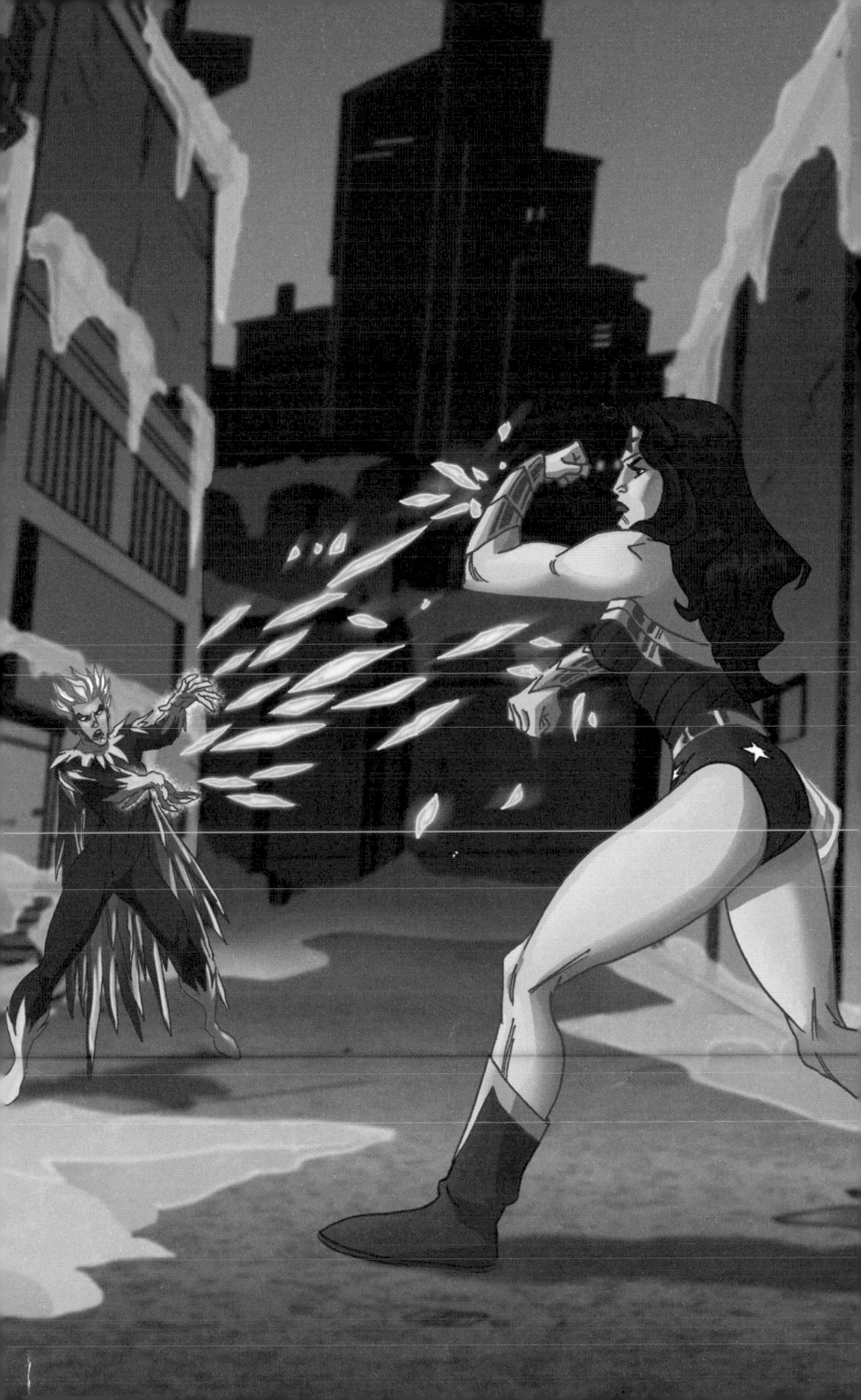

The Ice Pack quickly surrounded
the World's Greatest Heroes.

"We need a plan," said Wonder Woman.

"And fast!" added The Flash.

Batman spotted a manhole cover,

half hidden in the snow.

The Dark Knight removed the cover.

"Follow me," Batman said,

and then he leaped into the sewer.

The Ice Pack chased the three heroes
into the dark, steamy sewer.
They found only one—Batman!
"It's time to put an end
to this cold spell," he said.
Batman fired his grappling hook
through a manhole above his head.
He rocketed out of the sewer,
leaving the Ice Pack behind.

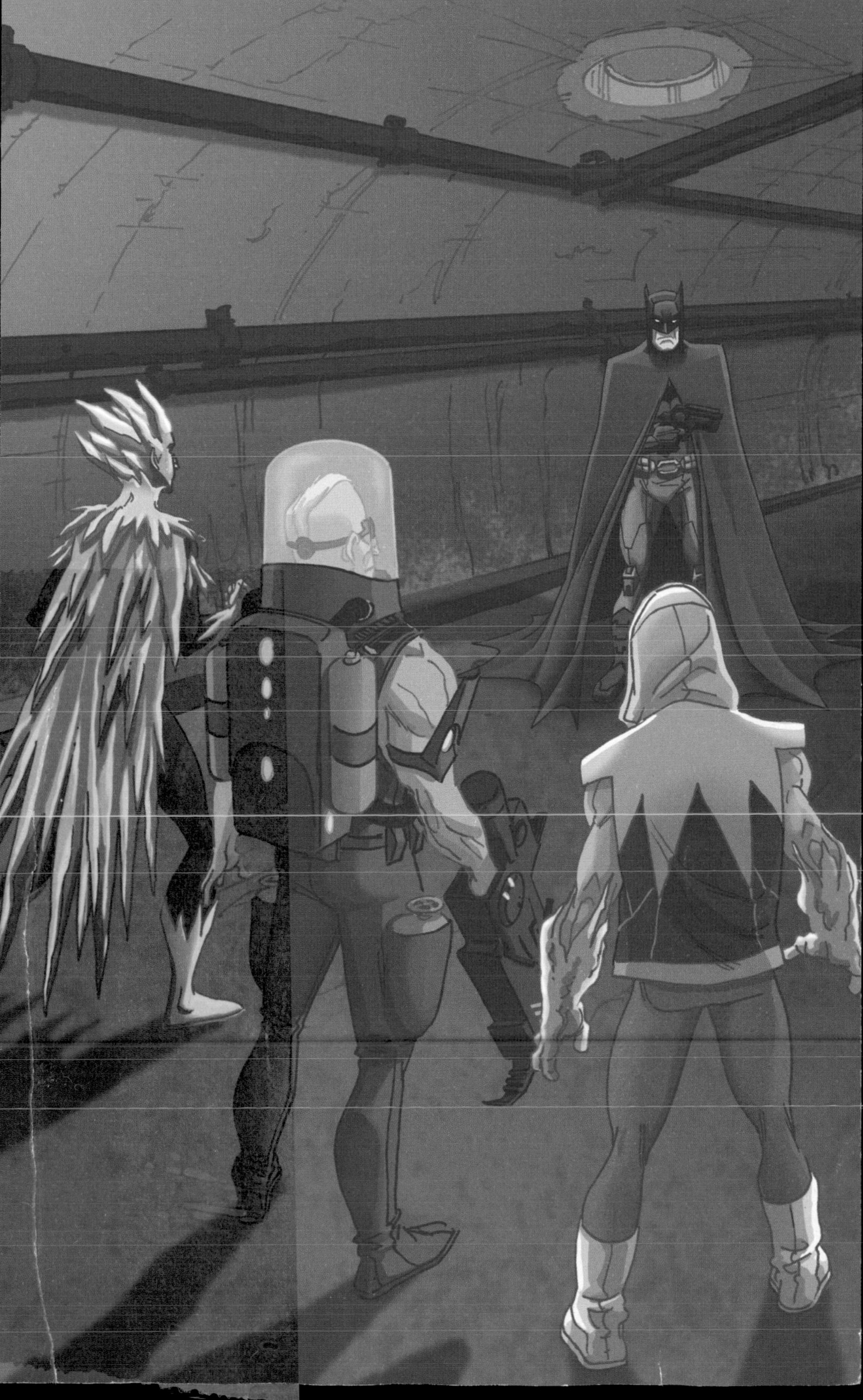

On the street, Wonder Woman sealed
the manhole with her super-strength.
Then The Flash sprinted
up and down the city street.

His lightning-quick legs melted
the snow beneath his feet.
Water flooded the storm drains.
It poured down on the Ice Pack
like wintery waterfalls.

Mr. Freeze started to panic.

"Chill!" Captain Cold commanded.

He was too late.

Mr. Freeze blasted his ray gun

into the neck-deep water.

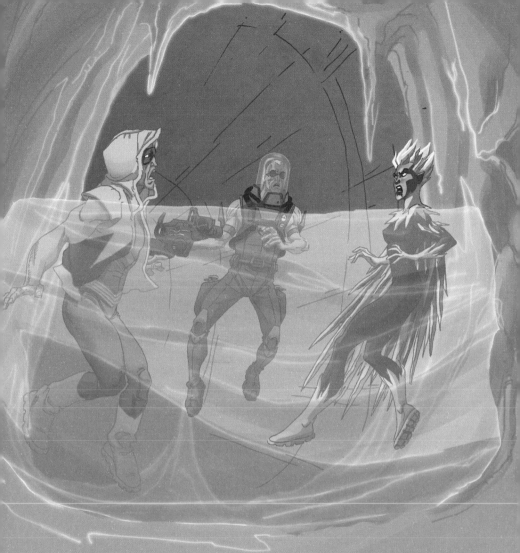

Instantly, the sewer water froze
into a solid block of ice.

Mr. Freeze, Captain Cold,
and Killer Frost were stuck inside.

Batman flung open the manhole,
and the Ice Pack shouted up at him.
"Wonder Woman," Batman began,
"would you help me
get these ice blocks
to a nice, warm cell block?"

"Sure thing," said Wonder Woman, heading toward her Invisible Jet. "And I'll do some spring cleaning," said The Flash.

A day later, Bruce relaxed in the sun outside Wayne Manor.

"Iced tea, sir?" asked the butler.

"I'd actually prefer it hot," Bruce said.